LEARN TO R

JONATHAN JAMES

SAYS

"Let's Be Friends"

by Crystal Bowman
illustrated by Karen Maizel

ZondervanPublishingHouse
Grand Rapids, Michigan

A Division of HarperCollins*Publishers*

Library of Congress Cataloging-in-Publication Data

Bowman, Crystal.
Jonathan James says, "Let's be friends" / by Crystal Bowman.
p. cm. — (Jonathan James)
Summary: Jonathan the rabbit discovers that he can be friends with
many kinds of people, from a boy in a wheelchair to a missionary who tells
people about Jesus.
ISBN: 0-310-49601-2
[1. Individuality—Fiction. 2. Physically handicapped—Fiction.
3. Wheelchairs—Fiction. 4. Christian Life—Fiction. 5. Rabbits—Fiction.]
I. Title. II. Series: Bowman, Crystal. Jonathan James.
PZ7.B6834Jp 1995
[E]—dc20   95-8053
                                                           CIP
                                                           AC

Edited by Lori J. Walburg and Leslie Kimmelman
Cover design by Steven M. Scott
Art direction by Chris Gannon
Illustrations and interior design by Karen Maizel

96 97 98 99 /❖ DP / 10 9 8 7 6 5 4 3

For Bill and Terri Howard
and my cousin Marion

—C. B.

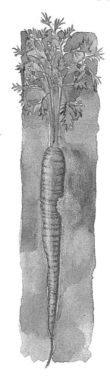

For Joanie,
my umbrella
—K. M.

CONTENTS

TOO SHORT

Jonathan James came home
from school.
He went right into his bedroom.

"Would you like a snack, J.J.?"
asked Mother.

"No," said Jonathan.

"Will you play with me?"
asked his little sister, Kelly.

"I don't want to play,"
Jonathan replied.

"Is something wrong?" asked Mother.

"Yes!" Jonathan exclaimed.

"I am too short.
I am shorter than all of my friends.
I don't like being short!"

"There is nothing wrong
with being short," said Mother.

"Be thankful that you are
strong and healthy."

"I *am* thankful
that I am strong and healthy,"
said Jonathan.
"But I am not thankful
that I am short."
"God made you
the way you are," Mother told him.
"You are special to Him,
and you are special to me."
Jonathan did not feel better.
He sat on his bed until dinnertime.

"Time to eat!" said Mother.

Jonathan didn't feel like eating.

He sat at the table

and looked at his food.

"I've been thinking," said Mother.

"I don't think you should

play with Jason anymore."

"Why not?" Jonathan asked.

"Jason wears glasses," said Mother.
"You don't want to play
with someone who wears glasses,
do you?"

"Jason is my best friend,"
Jonathan told her.
"I don't care that he wears glasses."

"Well," said Mother,
"you should not play with Matt.
His ears are too big."

"I like Matt," said Jonathan.
"He plays with me at recess.
I like his
big ears."

"Did you know that Mandi
lost her front tooth?" asked Father.
"No," said Mother.
"I didn't know that.
I guess Jonathan won't be playing
with her anymore."
"I like to ride bikes with Mandi,"
said Jonathan.
"She can ride her bike just fine
without that tooth."

"Well," said Mother.

"You don't mind

that Jason wears glasses.

And you like Matt,

even though he has big ears?"

"Yes," said Jonathan.

"And you still want to ride bikes

with Mandi?" Father asked.

"Yes, I do," said Jonathan.

"But maybe they won't want

to play with you," Mother said.

"Yes," said Father.

"Maybe they think you are too short."

"My friends don't care

that I am short," said Jonathan.

"They like me the way that I am."

"So do we," said Mother.

Jonathan smiled.

"So do I," he said.

Jonathan ate his dinner.

Then he went outdoors
to ride bikes with Mandi.

The next day,
Jonathan played
with Matt at recess.

And he walked home from school
with his best friend, Jason.
Jonathan liked his friends,
and they liked him.

THE VISITOR

"Why are you cleaning my room?"
asked Jonathan.
"And why is there
another bed in my room?"
"We are having a visitor,"
said Mother.
"Who?" asked Jonathan.
"Mr. Howard," said Mother.
"He is a missionary.
He tells people about Jesus."

Jonathan began to wonder:

What would Mr. Howard look like?

What kind of clothes would he wear?

"When is he coming?" Jonathan
asked.

"After dinner," said Mother.

"Where will he sleep?"
asked Jonathan.

"He is going to sleep
in your bed," said Mother.

"And you will sleep in the small bed."

Jonathan was not happy.

He did not want a missionary
staying at his house.

He did not want a missionary
sleeping in his bed.

That evening, the doorbell rang.

It was Mr. Howard.

Jonathan was surprised!

Mr. Howard looked nice.

He wore clothes just like

Father's clothes.

"Hello," said Mother and Father.

"Hello," Mr. Howard greeted them.

"This must be Jonathan."

"Hello, Mr. Howard," said Jonathan.

"You may call me Bill,"
said Mr. Howard.

"I will take your bags," Father
offered.

"Would you like to rest?"
Mother asked.

"Oh, no," said Bill.

"I am tired of sitting.
I would like to play outside.
Is there someone who could
play with me?"

"I will!" said Jonathan.

"Great!" said Bill.

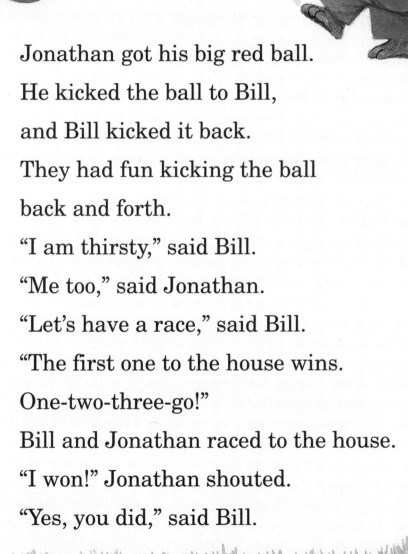

Jonathan got his big red ball.

He kicked the ball to Bill,

and Bill kicked it back.

They had fun kicking the ball

back and forth.

"I am thirsty," said Bill.

"Me too," said Jonathan.

"Let's have a race," said Bill.

"The first one to the house wins.

One-two-three-go!"

Bill and Jonathan raced to the house.

"I won!" Jonathan shouted.

"Yes, you did," said Bill.

They went into the house,
and Mother gave them lemonade.
Bill told Jonathan a story
about a little girl who lived far away.
She was very sick,
and her family was poor.
They could not buy medicine for her.
Bill brought her medicine,
and it made her better.

"Missionaries help people,"
Bill explained.

"And we tell them about Jesus."

"Maybe someday I will be a
missionary," Jonathan said.

"Maybe you will." Bill smiled.

Then he yawned.

"I am tired," said Bill.

"May I rest on the sofa?"

"Oh, no!" said Jonathan.

"Come to my room.

You can sleep in my bed,

and I will sleep in the small bed."

"That will be fun!" said Bill.

Jonathan showed Bill his room.

"What a nice bedroom!" Bill said.

"Thank you for sharing it."

"You're welcome," said Jonathan.

The next morning Bill said good-bye.

"I will miss you," said Jonathan.

"I will miss you too," said Bill.

"But we can write letters."

"Oh, yes!" Jonathan replied.

"We can't play ball in our letters,
but we can still be friends."

"We will always be friends," said Bill.

Jonathan smiled.

"Yes, we will," he agreed.

THE PICNIC

It was Saturday.

Jonathan and his family went
to the park for a picnic.

"Oh, look!" said Father.

"There is another family
having a picnic."

"Maybe we can share
our lunch with them," said Mother.

"Good idea," said Father.

Mother and Father said hello
to the other family.
They were nice.
They had a little girl
for Kelly to play with.
Her name was Sara.
Kelly and Sara went to play
on the swings.
They also had a boy
named Tommy.
Jonathan did not want
to play with Tommy.
Tommy sat in a wheelchair.
His legs were skinny.
He could not run or walk.
Jonathan decided to play
by himself.

"Why don't you play with Tommy?"
asked Father.
"I do not want to play
with Tommy," said Jonathan.
"He cannot run or walk.
It would not be fun
to play with him."
"God gave you strong legs,"
Father told him.
"You can run and walk
and even climb trees.
Why don't you find out
what Tommy can do?"
Jonathan went over to Tommy.
Tommy was making something
out of blocks.

"What are you making?"
Jonathan asked.

"I am making an airplane,"
Tommy explained.

"Wow!" said Jonathan. "Can I try?"

"Sure," said Tommy. "I'll help you."

Tommy helped Jonathan.

He even let Jonathan

put on the propellor.

"I know," said Tommy.

"Let's have a race."

"How?" asked Jonathan.

"See this button?" said Tommy.

Jonathan looked at the button
on Tommy's wheelchair.

"When I push the button
my wheelchair goes fast,"
Tommy explained.

"Let's race to the swings."

"Okay," Jonathan agreed.

Tommy pushed the button
on his wheelchair.

Jonathan ran beside Tommy.

Tommy got to the swings first.

"I won!" said Tommy.

"That was fun!" said Jonathan.

"Let's go on the merry-go-round,"
said Tommy.

"Okay," said Jonathan.

"Can you help me?" Tommy asked.

Jonathan helped Tommy
out of his wheelchair.

Tommy sat on the merry-go-round.

Jonathan pushed it hard
and jumped on.

The merry-go-round went fast.

Tommy and Jonathan went around
and around until they got dizzy.

"Time for lunch," called Mother.
Jonathan helped Tommy
get back into his wheelchair.
"Let's race again," said Jonathan.
"Okay," said Tommy.
"One-two-three-go!"
Jonathan and Tommy raced
to the picnic tables.
"I won!" said Tommy.
"You always win," said Jonathan.
Jonathan and Tommy
ate their sandwiches.

Soon it was time to go home.

Jonathan said good-bye to Tommy.

"I hope we can race again

sometime," said Jonathan.

"Me too," said Tommy.

"Maybe next time

I will even let you win!"

Jonathan laughed.

"I can't wait!" he said.

THE NEW NEIGHBOR

"Our new neighbors are here,"
said Jonathan.

"Oh?" said Mother.

"Come and see," said Jonathan.
"There is a big truck outside.
A man is bringing boxes
into the house."

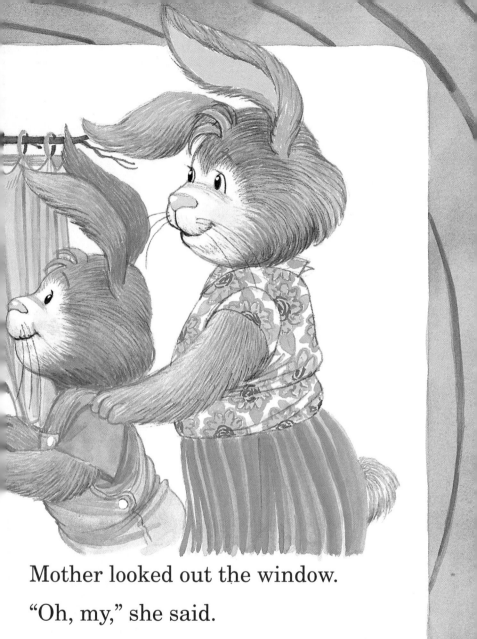

Mother looked out the window.

"Oh, my," she said.

"You are right.

Our new neighbors are here."

"May I go meet my new friend?"
asked Jonathan.

"What new friend?" asked Mother.

"My new friend next door,"
said Jonathan.

"How do you know
you will have a new friend?"
asked Mother.

"Because," said Jonathan,
"I asked God for a new friend.
God hears our prayers,
doesn't He?"

"Oh, yes," said Mother.

"God hears our prayers."

"Well, then," said Jonathan,

"may I go meet my new friend?"

"Yes." Mother nodded.

"You may go meet
your new friend."

Jonathan went outside.

He saw a man by the truck.

"Hello," said Jonathan.

"My name is Jonathan."

"Hello, Jonathan," the man replied.

"My name is George."

"Where is your boy?"
asked Jonathan.

"My boy is all grown up,"
said George.

"He doesn't live with me anymore."

"Oh," said Jonathan.

Jonathan was sad.

He wanted a new friend to play with.

"I could use your help," said George.

"You could?" asked Jonathan.

"Yes," said George, "follow me."

They went into the house.

George brought Jonathan some
boxes.

"There is a train set in these boxes,"
said George.

"If you unpack it,
we can put it together."

Jonathan unpacked
the train set.

There were lots of shiny cars
and a big, black engine.
George helped Jonathan
put the train together.
Soon the train was working.
It went around and around.
It even whistled!

Then it was time
for Jonathan to go home.
Jonathan said good-bye to George.
"Come back soon," George said.
"I have a bridge and a tunnel
for the train."
"I will," Jonathan promised.
Jonathan went home.

"Well," said Mother,

"did you meet your new friend?"

"Yes," said Jonathan.

"His name is George.

But he is not a boy."

"Is George a girl?" Mother asked.

"Oh, no!" laughed Jonathan.

"He is a nice man.

We played with his train set,

and he wants me to come again."

Mother smiled.

"I'm happy God heard your prayer," she said.

"Me too," said Jonathan.

"George will be a good friend."

READ UP ON THE ADVENTURES OF JONATHAN JAMES!

Jonathan James Says, "I Can Be Brave"

Book 1   ISBN 0-310-49591-1

Jonathan James is afraid. His new bedroom is too dark. He's going into first grade. And he has to stay at Grandma's overnight for the first time. What should he do? These four lively, humorous stories will show new readers that sometimes things that seemed scary can actually be fun.

Jonathan James Says, "Let's Be Friends"

Book 2   ISBN 0-310-49601-2

Jonathan James is making new friends! In four easy-to-read stories, Jonathan meets a missionary, a physically challenged boy, and a new neighbor. New readers will learn important lessons about friendship. And they will learn that our friends like us just for being who we are.

Jonathan James Says, "I Can Help"

Book 3   ISBN 0-310-49611-X

Jonathan James is growing up— and that means he can help! In four chapters written especially for new readers, Jonathan James learns to pitch in and help his family—sometimes successfully, sometimes not. Young readers will learn that they, too, have ways they can help.

Jonathan James Says, "Let's Play Ball"

Book 4   ISBN 0-310-49621-7

Jonathan James wants to learn how to play baseball. Who will teach him? Will he ever hit the ball? Four fun-filled chapters show young readers that, with practice, they too can succeed in whatever they try.

Look for all the books in the Jonathan James series at your local Christian bookstore.

📖 ZondervanPublishingHouse
5300 Patterson S.E. • Grand Rapids, MI 49530

Crystal Bowman lives with her husband and three children in Grand Rapids, Michigan. She is the author of *Cracks in the Sidewalk*, a humorous collection of children's poetry. "I love teaching children how to write funny poems," she says. Crystal enjoys snow skiing, eating frozen yogurt, and going to the beach.

Karen Maizel lives in Ohio with her husband, three daughters, and a dog, Oliver. She has always had a love for drawing and colors. "When I was a girl, my father saw how much I loved drawing," Karen says. "Even though we didn't have a lot of money, he took me to an art supply store two times and let me choose what I wanted. He showed me that my talent was important!"

Crystal and Karen would love to hear from you. You may write them at:

Author Relations
Zondervan Publishing House
5300 Patterson Ave., S.E.
Grand Rapids, MI 49530